Dear Parents:

Congratulations! Your child is taking the first steps on an exciting journey. The destination? Independent reading!

STEP INTO READING® will help your child get there. The program offers five steps to reading success. Each step includes fun stories and colorful art or photographs. In addition to original fiction and books with favorite characters, there are Step into Reading Non-Fiction Readers, Phonics Readers and Boxed Sets, Sticker Readers, and Comic Readers—a complete literacy program with something to interest every child.

Learning to Read, Step by Step!

Ready to Read   Preschool–Kindergarten
• big type and easy words • rhyme and rhythm • picture clues
For children who know the alphabet and are eager to begin reading.

Reading with Help   Preschool–Grade 1
• basic vocabulary • short sentences • simple stories
For children who recognize familiar words and sound out new words with help.

Reading on Your Own   Grades 1–3
• engaging characters • easy-to-follow plots • popular topics
For children who are ready to read on their own.

Reading Paragraphs   Grades 2–3
• challenging vocabulary • short paragraphs • exciting stories
For newly independent readers who read simple sentences with confidence.

Ready for Chapters   Grades 2–4
• chapters • longer paragraphs • full-color art
For children who want to take the plunge into chapter books but still like colorful pictures.

STEP INTO READING® is designed to give every child a successful reading experience. The grade levels are only guides; children will progress through the steps at their own speed, developing confidence in their reading. The F&P Text Level on the back cover serves as another tool to help you choose the right book for your child.

Remember, a lifetime love of reading starts with a single step!

*In honor of Abuelita Julia. I am proud to carry
your memories with me always.
—J.M.*

How to say the Spanish words in this book and what they mean:

Abuelita (ah-bweh-LEE-tah): grandmother
¡Aye yai yai! (EYE-yai-YAI): Oh no!
Delicioso/deliciosa (deh-lee-SYOH-soh/deh-lee-SYOH-sah): delicious
Feliz cumpleaños (feh-LEES koom-pleh-AH-nyohs): happy birthday
Mi hermana (mee ehr-MAH-nah): my sister
Mi prima (mee PREE-mah): my girl cousin
Niñas (NEE-nyahs): girls
Papi (PAH-pee): father
Pequeño (peh-KEH-nyoh): small
Sonrisa (sohn-REE-sah): smile
Tres leches cake (trehs LEH-chehs keyk): a sponge cake made with three kinds of milk
Una esponja gigante (OOH-na ehs-POHN-hah hee-GAHN-teh): a giant sponge
Uno, dos, tres, cuatro, cinco (OO-noh, DOHS, TREHS, KWAH-troh, SEENG-koh): one, two, three, four, five

Library of Congress Cataloging-in-Publication Data
Names: Mora, Julissa, author, illustrator.
Title: Baking with mi abuelita / written and illustrated by Julissa Mora.
Other titles: Baking with my grandmother
Description: First edition. | New York : Random House Children's Books, [2023] | Series: Step into reading | Audience: Ages 4–6. | Summary: Family members head into the kitchen to help Abuelita bake a tres leches cake for Papi's birthday.
Identifiers: LCCN 2022052086 (print) | LCCN 2022052087 (ebook) |
ISBN 978-0-593-65196-4 (trade paperback) | ISBN 978-0-593-65197-1 (library binding) |
ISBN 978-0-593-65198-8 (ebook)
Subjects: CYAC: Baking—Fiction. | Grandmothers—Fiction. | Hispanic Americans—Fiction. | LCGFT: Readers (Publications). | Picture books.
Classification: LCC PZ7.1.M66824 Bak 2023 (print) | LCC PZ7.1.M66824 (ebook) | DDC [E]—dc23

Printed in the United States of America
10 9 8 7 6 5 4 3 2 1
First Edition

This book has been officially leveled by using the F&P Text Level Gradient™ Leveling System.

Baking with Mi Abuelita

by Julissa Mora

Random House 🏠 New York

Abuelita loves to bake!
She makes the most
delicioso cakes.

It is Papi's birthday!
Mi hermana, mi prima,
and I will help Abuelita
bake a tres leches cake!

It will have

cherries on top!

"When your Papi
was pequeño,
he would help me bake
a tres leches cake.

"It was our
special tradition,"
Abuelita says.

Abuelita reads
the recipe.
"Making tres leches
is about measuring,"
she says.

We measure flour, salt,

baking powder,

and sugar.

"Making tres leches
is about counting,"
says Abuelita.
We count five eggs.
"Uno, dos, tres,
cuatro, cinco."

Crack! go the eggs.

We mix the batter.

Ew! The eggs are slimy.

I pour the batter
into the pan.

"Can we taste it now?"
I ask.
"Pretty please,
   with a cherry on top?"
"Not yet, niñas!"

Abuelita places the cake
in the oven
to bake.
Now we must wait!

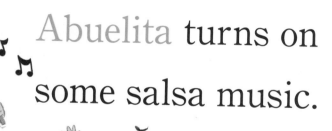

Abuelita turns on
some salsa music.

We dance!

We clean!

¡Ja! ¡Ja! ¡Ja!

We laugh!

Ding! Ding! Ding!

The cake is ready!

Papi pokes his head
into the kitchen.
"What is that sweet smell?"
Papi asks.
"It's a surprise!" we say.

"Who wants to take
the cake out of the pan?"
asks Abuelita.
"ME! ME! ME!"

I flip the cake over.
Part of it
sticks to the pan.

¡Aye yai yai!
Papi's birthday
is ruined!

"It's okay," says Abuelita.
"Making tres leches
is about patience."

Abuelita patches the cake back together.

Abuelita is our hero!

The next step is
my favorite part.
Now we add
the milk syrup
to the cake.

The cake
drinks it all up
like una esponja gigante.

At last, it's time
to make the icing.
Mix! Whip! Mix!

We spread it all over
the cake.

"Don't forget the cherries!" says Abuelita.

Papi pokes his head
into the kitchen again.
"Do I smell
tres leches cake?" he asks
with a big sonrisa.

"Surprise!"

We all shout,

"Feliz cumpleaños."

"Making tres leches

is about sharing,"

says Abuelita.

"Thanks for the deliciosa
birthday surprise!"
says Papi.
"Now you are part of
our special tradition, too."